LITTLE PEOPLE

A Fantasy Story
About Fathers, Sons, and Monsters

Daniel Charles Wild

For my dad, who released me into the wild.

"Ah, none of us really know our fathers."

– John Mulaney

CHAPTER 1

THE QUEST

My father hid a lot from us, and after he passed, some of his secrets came looking for me. Five days after his funeral, I dreamed about his train set—two small, plastic figurines from his diorama, to be more precise. When I woke up they were still there.

***

My father had loved two things: one was drinking, and the other was his diorama. Those were also the reasons my mom claimed she'd left him, but I knew it was more complicated. I knew I'd been the real reason.

My dad drank, sure. But he wasn't a drunk. He was a calm drinker, mostly. He'd drink and tinker away in his little world in the basement. My mom was annoyed with the drinking, with his hobby, his absence, and with him, but it could have gone on for years like that. It had gone on for years before I was born. But it came to a head when I was around four, and then it all got torn apart.

I had snuck into the basement and started playing with the model city. It looked like a toy world made just for me. I clamored up onto the table and towered over the town like a giant, laughing in amazement at the way the train sped around the track. As it came close to me, I grabbed the front car to make the train go faster. It flew off the track and into a row of perfect little buildings, the railroad cars buckling and folding behind it.

In my memory, the tiny toy people, all posed along the miniature Main Street, had scattered the moment before the train flew off the track, as if alive and trying to get out of the way. I laughed in surprise and stepped back, feeling something soft pop and smear beneath my heel. I slipped, tottered, and toppled backward onto a row of buildings and a tiny water tower.

When I fell, I felt things crunch beneath me and something wet explode against my back. I remember—though I must have imagined—a high-pitched chorus of tiny screams. Before I knew what was happening, I heard a roar, and I was suddenly flying, yanked up by my right arm.

My memory of the event is spotty. The figures darting, the screams—those things could have only happened in my four-year-old imagination. But the roar was real.

My dad was huge and terrifying as he lifted me into the air. I saw a sudden jumble of images: the miniature town spread beneath me, the figurines racing in all directions, my father's furious face in my peripheral vision, the harshness of the overhead light, the heel of my shoe kicking the light fixture and leaving a smear of something red. The terrible feeling of being pulled apart, the blinding pain in my arm and shoulder, seeing spots of darkness multiplying, and passing out.

My mom wouldn't talk much about it, but my sister did. She had opinions. She said my dad found me playing with his train set, and he hurt me to teach me a lesson. She said I was lucky I'd gotten away with just a broken arm. A few years earlier our cat, her cat really, got into the basement and must have made a mess. She heard our father screaming, and when she ran into the kitchen to see what was going on, he rushed up from the basement with the limp, bloody cat flopping in one white-knuckled hand and something else cupped tenderly in the other.

"He buried the cat in the backyard," she said.

She was sure he'd ripped the cat into two pieces. Tore off its head, she thought, because in the yard she saw a mound of dirt where the cat was buried, and a smaller mound beside it.

I didn't totally believe my sister's story, but I still remember the way she'd whispered it confidentially, her face so serious, her dark eyes wide. The way she kept glancing at my curled-up arm and looking away, embarrassed. I hadn't been torn in two, but I had been damaged. He said he hadn't meant to grab me so firmly, to yank me away so hard. I had just been so small, so easy to lift up. He was so sorry, he said. But it happened.

My shoulder had been dislocated, my dominant arm wrenched from its socket and badly broken. There was damage to the nerves and tendons and I never regained full use of it. Social workers got involved, my parents separated, my mom got full custody and everything else she asked for. He got the empty house he'd inherited from his father and the train set in the basement. He was left with the little world he loved, the one I had broken.

I remember my mom packing to leave. My arm in a cast, my right side hurting, I looked down at the two of them through the stairwell railing. He was crying, and sitting on the sofa with his face in his hands. From up there, he looked small and helpless, like one of the tiny toy people he was so protective of.

That's really all I remember about that time, my injury, and the divorce.

After a few years, I saw him again. First, there were supervised visits, and when I was older, it was one-on-one or with my sister too. It was always strained. It was rarely fun. It hurt him to see me, to see what he'd done in a moment of rage, to see me struggle to open a door or try to get a lid off a jar. I'd catch him looking at me with this stricken expression that I couldn't stand. He made me feel handicapped, flawed. He'd apologize too often, inevitably pour a drink from the cupboard above the sink, and then go to the basement, locking the door behind him and leaving my sister and me to entertain ourselves.

When my sister went to college, I stopped seeing my dad. It wasn't intentional, but it was easy. I didn't return a few calls, he gave up, and seven years went by.

And then he was gone.

***

Five days after his funeral, sleeping in my college apartment, I had the dream. In it, two plastic figures from the train set came to visit me.

They stood on the coffee table trying to get my attention, and I—lying on the sofa—was at eye level with them.

They held little paper horns, formed out of postage stamps, and they were bellowing through them, but I could barely hear them. I think this was the gist of it: that my father's miniature world was real, and it desperately needed my help. The train had stopped, the sun had been dark for a week, and now an unstoppable creature from the larger world was terrorizing the land.

I had stared at them blearily, rolled over, and fell back asleep.

When I woke up the next morning, I lay on the sofa in my college apartment, thinking about the dream, the diorama, and my father. When I rolled over, coffee table in my line of sight, I saw them. The figurines from the dream.

Both figures were lying on their backs. One was a farmer in overalls and a flannel shirt, and the other looked like a milkman; next to them, still curled at their edges, were the two stamps they'd been shouting through in my dream. I blinked hard a few times, and I laughed nervously, not sure I was awake, not believing they were in front of me.

I had been tangled in a blanket and lying on my left side with my good arm pinned beneath me, so I clumsily reached for one of the figures with my withered arm and twisted hand. Suddenly the tiny plastic milkman scrambled to his feet, and I jerked my hand back, the shock jolting me fully awake. He grabbed the curled postage stamp by his side and delivered two swift kicks to the farmer still lying down. Then the small, standing figure turned to face me, raising the funneled postage stamp to his tiny painted face.

And he started shouting.

It was a repeat of the points I'd heard in my dream—the dream I must still be having. I stared blankly at this tiny absurdity as he again launched into his high-pitched plea about my father's world needing help, the train wasn't running, the sun had gone out, and the monster was hunting in the darkness killing men, women, and children.

While the milkman shouted through his rolled-up stamp, his partner, who had stood up by this time, joined in with faint, affirmative outbursts of "That's right!" "Uh-huh!" and "Amen!" He was waving a crushed straw hat with one arm and clutching his presumably bruised ribs with his other. In his excitement, the farmer had forgotten to pick up his makeshift megaphone, and he stomped on the curled postage stamp as he hollered things I could barely hear.

I had to be dreaming still. But I felt awake. I could hear birds chirping outside and the whisper of cars driving by. My dreams didn't usually seem this real. Or maybe they did, and I just forgot when I woke up. This had to be a dream, an incredible one. I played along.

"How did you get here?" I asked, quickly lowering my voice to a whisper when the sound of my voice made them flinch and stagger backward.

"Your dad! Through the mail! He left our mayor envelopes, stamped and addressed, for when we'd need to reach you!" the milkman bellowed in reply.

Sure, I thought, that makes a strange kind of sense. It would be easier to reach me than my sister. I lived one town over, she lived across the country. Processing this, I started to sit up - pushing myself with the numb arm I'd been sleeping on. Reaching forward to steady myself, I accidentally jostled the coffee table with my clumsy right hand. Both toys scrambled to keep their balance. I felt a twinge of embarrassment at my clumsiness, and I mumbled an apology. I was off balance too. About as off balance as I'd ever been. Now sitting up, I looked down at them in dazed fascination, and they looked back at me.

I realized belatedly that sitting up so suddenly must have been a terrifying sight from their perspective. Both figures were about an inch tall, and they stared up at me with wide eyes. The milk-man, the leader of the two, smiled slightly and squinted up. But the farmer clutched his straw hat to his chest and slid behind the milkman, his mouth a tiny painted O. He's scared. I scared him.

That realization struck me as both pitiful and hilarious, and I covered my mouth with my hands to muffle a bark of laughter. Maybe this isn't a dream. Maybe I'm having a psychotic break. I'm hallucinating here in my living room.

I stared down at the figures, they stared up at me, and I surprised myself by starting to cry, just a little. Maybe it was the shock of seeing them, maybe it was from trying to hold back my laughter, or maybe I was just going crazy. But the feeling of my eyes starting to well up, seeing the two visitors start to blur in my vision, snapped me out of my impending laughing fit and brought me back to the moment.

"So, you want me to go to my dad's house, turn on the basement light, and start the electric train again?" I asked softly to break the silence, already knowing their answer.

"Yes! And kill the monster!" The milkman piped up in response, and the farmer hiding behind him chimed in with an emphatic "Yes siree!" But he didn't sound quite as enthusiastic as he had before. He sounded afraid.

"Sure, why not," I replied, shaking my head in disbelief. "I can do that for you. Yeah, let's do this." Then I started to laugh in earnest, rubbing tears out of my eyes while the two tiny men looked up at me with matching expressions of perplexity, perplexity bordering on fear.

CHAPTER 2

VOYAGE AND RETURN

Before leaving my apartment, I secured the two of them in a makeshift carrying case, with their permission. It was an empty plastic margarine container with a wad of toilet paper as padding and holes punched in the lid. I questioned if the plastic really needed airways if they too were made of plastic, but they insisted.

Leaving the apartment with the container firmly gripped in my good hand, I glanced at my mailbox. A red string hung from just under the lid all the way to the porch, swaying slightly in the fall breeze. With my bad hand, I propped open the lid and pulled the string to hear the jangle of a key ring. One of the keys was new—

freshly cut and shining brightly. The second was ancient, a heavy, pitted black skeleton key with a railroad crossing sign painted on its bow. I had never seen it before, but I knew what door it opened.

I peered over the lid of the mailbox and reached in to find an envelope. A white envelope with the corner torn open, my dad's address in the other corner, and three rough patches where stamps had been peeled off. Huh. They weren't kidding. Inside was an empty matchbox, lined with a cotton ball. If this is how talking toys traveled, it must have been cramped.

It made sense to me at this point—as much as a dream can make sense—that they had arrived in the letter, shimmied down the string, and squeezed under my front door. Looking down, I saw specks of blood on the porch, and a few small bloodied feathers that I must have stepped over on the way out. Following the spots, I saw that just inside the door, laid out across the doorstop, was a third figurine.

I crouched down to get a closer look. It was a little businessman in a blue suit stained nearly black with blood. His face and torso were covered with—an American flag? no, wait—the third postage stamp, and his body was sprinkled with bits of feather. I lifted the stamp to see his arms crossed over his chest and cradling a tiny, bloodstained nail that nearly spanned the length of his figure. In his arms, it looked like a spear.

Three little adventurers tucked themselves into the matchbox, and only two made it into my apartment alive. Judging by the feathers, I could only assume it was a bird. They fought, one fell, and the two survivors must have laid their friend to rest on the burial slab of my doorstop.

I stood up, and standing in the doorway, turned to survey my apartment. I could imagine the route the two of them must have taken. Leaving their friend behind, they made the long trek from the entryway to the plateau of my coffee table. They navigated past my kicked-off shoes, resting by the door like sleeping sentinels. They must have circumvented the hills of the rumpled coat I'd tossed on the floor, and hiked past the monuments of junk scattered around my small apartment.

When they eventually reached the coffee table next to the sofa where I was sleeping, they had scaled one of its legs—as evidenced by two shiny nails left at the base, weapons they discarded to make the climb. I could see that the tips were filed down to sharp points, and both were streaked with drying blood.

The two of them laid down their arms, climbed up into the sky, and clambered up to a new world. They walked defenseless across the checkered tile surface of the table, around the pile of textbooks, a collapsing stack of DVDs, and a few empty glasses crowded together like a crystal city. They were small tourists, stepping through an odd landscape of huge and miscellaneous things.

In the sky above them, the ceiling fan whirled at the top of the world, like a strange and bladed constellation. I imagined them using the vast horizon of my sleeping form as a reference, walking on until, at last: the three of us were face to face. With a canyon between us, their tiny, determined faces looked up at my giant one, they formed their stamps into funnels, and started shouting.

They had been on an odyssey, I now realized, and they lost one along the way. All because they needed someone to simply flip a switch, and turn on a trainset. It was a lot to process. I was determined to help.

There was something else in the letter too—a note from my father.

If you're reading this, you've learned there is a world that needs to be protected. The house belongs to you and your sister now. Before you do anything, visit the mayor of the basement. He'll explain everything.

—Dad

I looked at the margarine container with its two tiny travelers in my left hand, and then at the short—much too short—letter from my father in my twisted right hand. I had a lot of questions for my dad. Questions I'd never get to ask him. I felt my eyes start to sting, and my shoulder twinged.

Lacking the dexterity in my right side to fold the letter one-handed, I crumpled it and clumsily shoved the balled-up paper in my pocket. It took two tries to get it in. As was often the case when I thought about my father, I couldn't tell if I was sad or angry. That's another thing, for better or worse, that I'd never be able to talk to him about.

I'd have to settle for talking to the mayor.

Driving to my father's house was surreal. I put the plastic container on top of my coat on the floor in front of the passenger seat. That seemed as safe a place as any for the two little guys. I found myself driving more cautiously than usual. I didn't want to get in an accident and have the milkman and farmer bouncing around. After seeing the businessman's corpse, I was aware of their vulnerability.

I also didn't want to get pulled over. I didn't want a police officer seeing the container on the floor and suspiciously asking me to show him its contents. Though surely the two of them would freeze if that happened, that they'd know to play plastic. I felt confident the milkman would do that. I wasn't so sure about the farmer. I should have said something about that to them. I would if I saw lights in the rearview.

I was driving slow mostly because I still wasn't convinced I wasn't dreaming all this. A good rule of thumb I just made up: if you think you might be hallucinating, drive carefully. Maybe I had been seeing things. Two little things, about an inch high. Maybe getting a letter from my dead dad with the keys to his house while I was half asleep had rattled me into imagining the rest.

That actually made a lot of sense and seemed more and more likely as I drove down one familiar midwestern street after another. By the time I arrived at my dad's house, I was sure that was the case. But I had to check. I nervously peeled off the lid of the container, and there they were—the milkman and the farmer, rising unsteadily to stand at attention on the toilet paper. Both of them stared up at me expectantly, their eyes wide and mouths in tight, determined smiles. I smiled back a little shakily, feeling unsteady myself.

"Here we are, guys," I said quietly, nervously looking to see if any of my father's neighbors were around to see me talking into a margarine container. Thankfully, we were alone.

The shiny key opened the back door, and I walked into my childhood kitchen. Nostalgia descended on me like a weight. It was a physical force all around me, up my nose, in my head, in my chest. The kitchen smelled like him—cigarettes, Brut aftershave, and very faintly, the sharp smell of the unidentified liquor he drank. I hadn't been here for seven years, and I hadn't missed it. It was almost exactly the way I remembered it, just a little smaller, more bare, and a little more run down. A bubble of sadness threatened to rise in me. It felt a little like vertigo, a little like desperation, and a lot like fear. I forced it down and tried not to think about it.

Across the kitchen I could see the door to his basement. It seemed warped by the weight of memories. According to my sister, it was the door he'd burst through with the cat he'd killed and the son he'd broken. It was the closed door he hid behind for years, the door that kept him from us.

I felt a sudden sharp ache in my right side, a twinge that ran from my shoulder to my fingertips. I gripped the key ring as tight as I could with my weaker and smaller hand. Then holding the container securely in my good hand, a small chariot with its gladiators peering over the rim, I advanced through the kitchen with the skeleton key extended before me like a sword. If this was a dream, it was frighteningly vivid. It all seemed dangerously real.

I tried the basement door. Locked. I inserted the skeleton key into the lock, and it seemed to sink all the way in, slipping from my fingertips like a quarter being deposited in a game at an arcade. I clumsily grasped at the keyhole, patting at the lock ineffectually with my pinching fingertips. The key ring, with its a lone house-key, fell straight down, clattering on the grimy kitchen tile.

I looked down at the floor for the skeleton key. It had to have fallen. No sign of it. Stupidly, I looked again at my empty right hand with its gnarled fingers reflexively pinching at the empty air. The key wasn't there either.

I stared down at the key ring on the floor with its single jutting house key sticking out like a middle finger. The fact that the key to the basement, railroad bow and all, had seemingly, impossibly, slipped off of the ring and been sucked into the keyhole like a spaghetti noodle, lurched me out of the fugue state I'd slipped into. I tried the doorknob again. The door was still locked, and the key had disappeared.

Confused and panicked, I jerked my head from left to right, scanning the floor for the key. I became aware that the milkman was yelling and leaning his upper body too far over the rim of the container while the farmer held on to him, waving his arms and trying to get my attention.

"The key's in the workshop! It's waiting! But to open the door, you need to pour a drink from the bottle in the cupboard!" The milkman shouted, gesturing with both arms towards the cupboard above the sink.

I looked at him blankly, feeling a dawning apprehension. Déjà vu overtook me as I slowly turned toward the cupboard looming over the rust-stained kitchen sink. I saw my right hand, moving autonomously, reaching for the cupboard's handle. Then opening it, reaching in, and with a dexterity I didn't know it had, pinching the rim of a tumbler and pulling it down to the counter with a clink. I reached for the familiar brown bottle waiting in the cupboard's depths. I grasped it with a confidence I didn't feel, placed it beside the tumbler, and twisted off its cap. I poured two fingers of the auburn liquid with its familiar biting smell. Then I set the bottle down next to the tumbler and twisted the cap back on with a quick, unusually fluid motion of my right hand.

As I screwed on the lid, I heard a muffled click inside the lock of the basement door. I felt my body stiffen, and I turned to stare at the door. It cracked open on its own like a dark vertical mouth about to speak. It waited patiently. I glanced back at the bottle and noticed the yellowing label featured a illustration of a old fashioned train pulling out of a station, and that the bottle was still filled to the brim—nearly overflowing. The level of liquid hadn't gone down at all.

A cold sweat broke out across my forehead. My right hand, which had performed the trick with the glass and bottle with such unfamiliar grace and strength, suddenly felt weak and started to shake.

The bottle, the glass, the sharp smell of the liquor, the open basement door —it was all too terribly familiar. I felt like my dad was in the room. I looked down imploringly at the milkman and the farmer, who were watching with solemn expressions from the plastic peanut gallery seating cupped in my other hand.

"I won't drink it," I said, in a voice that sounded surprisingly childlike and plaintive to my ears.

"It's not for drinking," the milkman shouted back faintly, his voice sounding a little hoarse.

"It's for the workshop!" the farmer chimed in.

Too far into this to turn back now, I grasped the tumbler with my right hand, held their container securely with my left, and nudged the basement door wider with my foot. Light from the kitchen window behind me illuminated a spinning galaxy of dust motes and the steps leading to the basement. The skeleton key wasn't on the top step, as I really hoped it would be. At the bottom of the stairs, I could see a dull glow, pulsing like emergency lights.

I descended into the darkness tentatively. I felt a slight vertigo and with both hands full I couldn't use the handrail, so I leaned against the wall as I took the first few steps. I'd only been down here once before, and as much as I would have liked to, I could never forget the layout. The stairway opened to the finished half of the basement on the left, and to the right, a sliding door lead to the unfinished half of the basement and my father's workshop.

As I made my way down, I recognized the glow as Christmas lights. They covered the ceiling, faintly illuminating my father's diorama—or what it had become. Instead of the single table from my four-year-old memory, it had expanded—an endless surface across the entire room, overtaking the basement. I stood silently with my two plastic friends and could hear a faint rustling, like leaves in the wind.

I squinted in the dim light at the ceiling. Among the twinkling lights were glow-in-the-dark stars and a few odd shaped lumps dangling from string. In the center, there was a ceiling fan with a single large bulb and model planes hanging from its blades. The barely illuminated landscape unrolled beneath it all, seemingly climbing up the walls.

"Holy shit," I breathed.

I patted at the wall frantically with the back of my hand holding the tumbler, looking for the switch I'd been summoned to flip. I had to see more. I had to see it better.

"The switch is at the bottom of the steps," said the milkman. "Careful where you're stepping!"

Right as he said that, I saw the switch a few steps down and underneath it, on the first step, built up about two feet, was a delicate scaffolding, made of matchsticks, toothpicks, duct tape, and string. It was partially smashed and sagging, the crude construction materials scattered at its base.

"We tried to flip the switch ourselves, but the monster attacked," the milkman shouted.

"Killed 'em, ate 'em too!" the farmer added, fear in his voice.

In the flickering gloom from the Christmas lights, I could see dark stains smeared on the floor, streaked and speckled on the wall, like a psychotic child's scrawl. Distracted by these thoughts, I felt something crunch beneath my descending foot. Grimacing with disgust, I told myself it was a toothpick and continued down the last few steps, watching where I stepped and holding the tumbler out before me. Then, as though making a toast, I used the rim of the glass to push up the switch and flip on the light.

My eyes, accustomed to the dark, narrowed at the flash of light.

For a moment, I felt like I had been transported outside and hundreds of feet into the air. The diorama hadn't simply expanded to more tables; the whole room was the diorama. The basement floor had been painted green, the walls and ceiling robin's egg blue. The shapes hanging from the ceiling were masses of cotton, and looked like floating cumulonimbus clouds. The ceiling fan's bulb was the room's white sun, and as it switched on, the fan's bright yellow blades spun slowly around, and the suspended planes started to fly, spinning in wide, lazy circles with the gentle centripetal force.

Below the facsimile of the sky, the model world spread out across a large, elevated island in the room's center, connected by railroad track to sturdy tables along the room's perimeter.

On the left side of the room, the track cut through a dense, old-growth forest dotted with tiny log cabins. The forest expanded up the side of a papier-mâché mountain range—taller than me—that sloped up against the wall. The mountains were topped with sheer white peaks, dotted with igloos and frosted with artificial snow.

The far table was a vast sandbox desert, with a scattering of quaint adobe huts, hand-stacked stones, artificially weathered rock formations, cacti, palm trees, dunes, a pyramid, and faux red stone cliffs. In the opposite corner, an old-timey train station was surrounded by wooden buildings, making a scene straight out of a western.

Along the right wall was a jungle in miniature. The table

exploded with plants beneath a sun lamp that came on when I flipped the switch. Among the foliage I could see straw huts, small stone animal sculptures, an overgrown temple, and a large stone Buddha sitting placidly against the wall with its arms and legs folded and its eyes closed.

Below the ceiling fan was the centerpiece, a three-level island. Two hinged bridges connected this center table to the little worlds around the perimeter. The top of the island was covered nearly end to end with a tiny, picturesque town, encircled by a train track. In contrast to its perfect houses lining perfect streets was a wall along the edges, standing about four inches high and constructed crudely out of Legos, toothpicks, foam peanuts, and pieces of cardboard.

This model town, unbelievably realistic, felt like it landed here from the 1950s. The town center featured a working bubbling fountain that had come on with the switch. In the center of the fountain, a brass statue of a medieval knight in armor, smeared with paint, stood on an elevated platform. One of its hands was clenched into a fist and resting on its breastplate, the other was triumphantly holding a sword toward the light.

On one side of the fountain was a second train station, and on the other side, the square opened up to a little Main Street. Spreading out from the center of town were stores, buildings, and idyllic homes. In the corner farthest from me was a park peppered with benches, trees, and bushes. Closer to me were a few factories, a railyard with a hanger, a few disconnected train cars, and two antique trains, neither of which were on the tracks.

The level of detail, and the amount of work it must have required to create it, was breathtaking. Taking it all in, I staggered back against the wall, and my heel accidentally crushed a section of the partially constructed scaffolding under the light switch. I felt a twinge of guilt but couldn't stop staring at the world my father had so painstakingly created.

I traced the tracks with my eyes, imagining the route the train must traverse. The island was elevated. Under the top level were two more levels. The second and third levels were in the shadows, but I could see a few things. On the first level, the spiraling track looped around the town, and then through a subway station cut into the tabletop, descended to the second level, where it looped around and then crossed one of the up-sloped bridges and traversed the three tables along the walls, the forest, desert, and jungle. It would then complete its circuit, returning once more to the town center by way of the second bridge.

The second level was in the shadows, but I could make out a castle and the interior of a cave with stained stalactites and stalagmites. Another section looked like a futuristic city made of discarded computer parts and tinfoil. There was an aquarium filled with water—at the top, a floating toy boat, and at the bottom, a sunken pirate ship and treasure chest. That was just what I could see from the stairs—there was even more I couldn't.

The bottom level was filled with miscellaneous stuff. There were foam planets with hooks on the top, waiting to be hung; a few unfinished nature scenes; partially constructed model cars and planes; an overturned battleship. I could also see broken and discarded diorama sections, art supplies, cans of paint, bundles of wire, rolls of foil, a stack of craft magazines, unlabeled boxes, and plastic bins. The entire bottom layer was also lightly covered with cobwebs and dust.

My eyes were drawn back to the wall around the town. Like the scaffolding I had just stepped on, it had not been created with the same attention to detail. The opening in the wall where the train track ran through it had been barricaded by a door of reinforced toothpicks, that when moved aside would allow the train to enter the railyard. Then the train would travel through the town, looping around the table-top to repeat the process again. Its path was a triple infinity symbol, across two levels and three climates. It was ingenious. But where was the train?

As I was staring, the town suddenly stirred. Tiny figures, hundreds, maybe a thousand or more, poured out of the buildings around the square, surging toward the plaza around the fountain at the base of the statue. Over the soft sound of the water running, I could hear something—was it static? No, I realized, it was the roar of the crowd cheering and applauding. I wondered if it was for me, or for the two adventurers who had successfully returned with me in tow.

"Take us to the statue!" The milkman shouted, his voice now hoarse. "The mayor will explain everything!"

CHAPTER 3

THE TRAGEDY

I drifted toward the island as though in a dream, my eyes hungrily scanning the town. I noticed additional details everywhere I looked. What looked picture perfect from afar was much more interesting up close. The streets were painted with abstract patterns, and the buildings' walls were covered with intricate murals in different shapes and colors. It looked like comic book art. Each mural featured a knight in armor—the knight from the fountain. His armor was painted differently in each one, but in all of them, he was wielding his sword and battling monsters.

In the mural on the hardware store, he was leading a group of soldiers into battle against a wave of spiders. The soldiers by his side seemed tiny in comparison. None reached higher than his knee, but armed with sharpened nails, they fought spiders as large as they were. In the center of the painting, the knight was fighting the largest spider of them all, and he was immortalized in the act of spearing its bloated abdomen.

In another mural, the knight was swarmed by black crickets, each one easily the length of his leg. He was depicted caving in the face of one with his clenched, gauntleted fist, his sword above his head, about to descend on another like a bolt of lightning.

I scanned over the crowd, in a third painting, the knight grappled with two savage-looking field mice, each half his size. He was choking the life out of one with his armored forearm and was about to bring his sword down on the head of the other.

The knight's visor was raised in these paintings, showing the strong-jawed face of a superhero. With a shock of recognition, I realized that although stylized, idealized—it was my father. My father was their savior; my father was their hero.

But not all of the murals showed him winning.

In one painting, the knight was screaming in apparent terror. He gripped the handle of his sword with both hands, staring up at an enormous cat that held a young girl's bleeding body in its mouth. The girl's head was twisted at an odd angle, her dark eyes glazed over, her dark hair hanging limply, and a long rope of blood dangled from her mouth. It was disturbing—even more so that the girl looked like my sister.

In another mural, the knight was disarmed, sprawled on his stomach in the foreground. A giant rampaged through the town behind him, with odd proportions that made it look like an enormous child. The knight was staring at the viewer—staring at me—and weeping. Behind him, the train was off the tracks, its cars scattered like a child's toys. Towering above this scene, against the town's skyline, the giant child laughed maniacally. Under his huge descending foot, two figures cowered. A woman, with long dark hair like my mother, raised a protective arm and held a dark-haired boy in the other. The boy, who stared up wide-eyed in terror, looked familiar too. The giant loomed over them, frozen before he brought his foot down. Behind his huge form waited a fragile water tower, and next to it, a house that looked just like the one I was in.

Both the boy and the giant looked like younger versions of me, though the giant's laughing face was utterly grotesque—warped by a psychotic maliciousness. In the far background of the painting, looming in the clouds, an even larger figure reached for the smaller giant with hands desperately extended. But it was too far away to save the tiny mother and child paralyzed in the growing shadow of the giant's foot.

The painting was a startling version of the last time I had been in the basement. I remember crashing the train, stepping on something, and crushing the water tower and house with my fall. What I didn't know then is what—no, who—my father was trying to protect as he yanked me into the air. As a child, I had terrorized this town and caused the deaths of an unknown number of its occupants.

I felt my eyes start to sting. I had to make this right somehow.

As the teeming crowd parted, cheering all the while, I lowered the margarine container like a descending UFO next to the statue of my father.

The crowd swarmed it, a few figures leaping in to hug the farmer and milkman and help them out. They lifted both figures onto their shoulders, roaring approvingly. Bending down for a closer look, I could see that their faces, the milkman and the farmer too, were laughing and crying. My two transports had their arms raised victoriously, both of them stars in this impossible impromptu parade of little people.

I smiled at the spectacle, overwhelmed by the chaos. There were tiny men, women, and children of all ages. Some wore crisp suits and skirts like everyday husbands and wives from the 1950s town, but there were other costumes too—plumbers, policeman, waiters, bellhops, construction workers, teenyboppers, and more. There were settlers, cowboys, gunslingers, bartenders, Indians, prospectors, hunters, and Eskimos draped in fur. I saw Aztec warriors in elaborate feathered outfits, Buddhist monks in orange robes, and African tribesman standing side-by-side with characters that looked like they had stepped out of a Renaissance Fair. There were army soldiers from different eras, people in futuristic costumes, figures in swimwear, and a few figures in antique diving suits. It was the wildest, happiest, and most diverse crowd I'd ever seen.

As I stared down grinning like an idiot, my eyes met the milkman's. Bouncing on the shoulders of his fans, he grinned and pointed at me with both arms. He was mouthing something, I don't know what, but it didn't matter. I could see the joy on his face, raw, pure, and directed at me. I nodded back, and smiling widely, held up the tumbler still gripped in my hand. I was toasting him, the farmer, and the fallen businessman, on their success, on bringing me here to turn on the sun and bring back the wind. They were the real heroes; I was just happy I'd been able to help. But, our adventure wasn't over yet. I still needed to restart the train, and they had a monster they needed help defeating. I glanced back at the murals, focusing on the one of the knight—no, my father—killing the mouse.

I couldn't wait.

Eventually, when the crowd quieted down and drew back, I got to meet the mayor. Dressed like a carnival barker, he was the oldest figurine I'd seen so far. His paint was worn off in places, and he hunched over, using a broken toothpick for a cane. As he hobbled across the square, the milkman and the farmer, who I noticed had lost his hat, walked slowly beside him.

They helped him make his way to the fountain's edge and sit down beneath the towering knight. A little dark-haired girl trailed the three of them, carrying a stack of stamps. A tiny black dog with a wagging tail followed the child. This was the first animal I'd seen in the diorama. It seemed oblivious of me, looming over the horizon, but I could see its head moving left to right and up and down, watching every gesture of the three men and the child.

I found a stool under one of the tables along the wall and pulled it up to the center island. The crowd murmured at the sounds the stool made as it scraped against the floor, and the dog started barking. I wondered briefly if it sounded like thunder to them, and I vowed to be more careful. Then I sat down, leaning over the town, with my ear as close to the little ensemble as possible, and asked what I could do to help.

Communicating was difficult, even with the stamps rolled into megaphones. Both the milkman and the farmer's voices were starting to give out. The mayor wasn't able to talk very loudly either, and the child didn't talk at all. But the dog was able to generate a surprising amount of volume. When I leaned in, it noticed me with a vengeance, and raised a frantic ruckus until the child picked up the dog and soothed it in her arms, burying her face in its fur.

Despite these communication challenges, the mayor, with the milkman and farmer's help, conveyed what their last week had been like. My father had been experiencing pain in his right shoulder and arm, they said, that spread to his chest. Alarmed, he called the paramedics and went outside. In his urgency, he must have left the front door slightly ajar as he staggered toward the wicker chair on the porch. The milkman, who was in the habit of spending time upstairs, watched him with concern from the living room window. He said my father had waited for the ambulance, grimacing and holding his clenched right hand against his chest. Then his hand relaxed, and he lowered his chin to his chest and slouched in his wicker chair. Distraught, the milkman slid down the curtain and ran toward the basement to share the terrible news.

Their father was dead.

As he made the long descent down the basement stairs, he suddenly saw the skeleton key fly over his head like a comet, making its way toward its hook in the workshop. But, the front door was still open.

Eventually someone, a mailman, a neighbor, maybe my mother stopping by to pick a suit for the funeral, had shut and locked the front door. But something hungry from the outside had already gotten in the house, and it made its way to the basement.

The mayor said that my father had been preparing the diorama's inhabitants for his absence for a while. He explained that if something happened to him, the key to the basement would return to the workshop on its own.

Once that happened, he hoped my sister or I would eventually visit the house. If we didn't, the little people would need to mail the skeleton key and a house key in one of the envelopes he prepared. He recommended they try me first. I was closer. I could get there faster. If the key returned without me, they should mail it to my sister. If it returned without her, then they should try to send it to me again.

The key would always return, and eventually my sister or I would return with it. The house was our responsibility, and one of us would take care of the things that the little people couldn't handle on their own. We had to. We had the same father. We were family.

They had been prepared to wait for weeks for one of us to arrive. My father had paid off the house; the bills were handled by a trust. The townspeople had enough supplies to last for years, and the sun bulb would last for decades. They had talented builders, and plenty of supplies—they even built the scaffolding to turn the sun on and off on their own. What they hadn't been prepared for was an unstoppable killer from the outside, invading their world on the heels of our father's death.

It snuck into the basement while the overhead light was off for the service they held for my father. After seeing the key streaking through the sky, and then hearing the milkman's account of what had happened, almost all of the diorama's inhabitants had ridden the train to the town center to attend. The only ones not in attendance had been the builders dispatched to the scaffolding beneath the switch to wait for the mayor's signal.

They had been instructed to turn on the light at the end of the service, when the engineer blew the train whistle three times.

The small team stood hand in hand, mourning together under the switch and waiting in the dark for the lonely sound of the train whistle. The monster reached them first. It attacked, slaughtered the builders by the light switch, and damaged the carefully con-structed scaffolding in the process.

After the ceremony around the fountain, the mayor, his face wet with tears, looked over the crowd of solemn faces illuminated by the flickering Christmas lights strung overhead. He gestured to the engineer waiting in the idling train across the plaza. The whistle blew three times—but the sun didn't come on.

Confused, but not yet alarmed, the mayor dispatched a caravan of the town's fastest runners to the construction site beneath the light switch to see what was the problem. The group of four in-cluded an Indian runner and his young daughter in training. Only the daughter made it back to the town alive. Something had killed the other runners, yanking them one by one into the darkness as the child raced across the basement floor toward the island.

Traumatized, the girl somehow made it back alone, and climbed up to the town on a piece of knotted string left dangling for the runners' return. A young soldier, patrolling the tabletop's perimeter for spiders, had found the her curled up in a ball at the very edge. She had been nearly unconscious, covered with some-one else's blood, with strands of course gray hair in one tightly clenched fist.

When questioned about what she'd seen, she wouldn't say a

word. The soldier who brought the her into town claimed that when he carried the girl past the murals, she had screamed, pointed at the painting of the knight fighting the mice, and then burst into tears. Since then, the child, who had a knack for drawing, had drawn a mouse several times. In each drawing, it was enormous, the size of a house, shown dismembering bodies, biting off heads, and tearing people in half. The child had turned the creature that had killed her father and the other runners into something impossibly demonic.

The mayor, disturbed by the drawings and full of pity for the child, took the art supplies away. Not wanting to panic the people of the town, he then tore up the drawings. But he still thought about them—the jagged lines of bristling fur, the long yellow incisors, the muzzle stained with blood, and the black pits of its eyes. A child's imagination could be a disturbing thing.

The mayor and the soldiers knew what they were dealing with—a mouse, or even worse, mice—particularly savage with a taste for human blood. They had dealt with mice before. Mice were terrifying creatures that could grow up to three times the size of a grown man in their world, four times if you counted the tail. They were scared of the light, but in the dark they were fearless. They were also incredibly fast, hard to kill, and if they weren't exterminated, they bred fast too. A breeding pair could overrun the basement within months. Then they'd have a war on their hands. A war they couldn't win.

The mayor knew they would likely need to send for help, but he also knew it could take awhile for my sister or me to arrive. Typically they'd summon the knight to battle something like this, but that wasn't an option at the moment. They had to do something now, before they had a litter to deal with. The knight had killed the adult field mice that had invaded the basement three years back, but the most experienced soldiers believed they could have handled it themselves by sheer numerical superiority. Now they had a chance to test that theory. They loaded up the train with a platoon of their bravest men and hunting dogs that had smelled the hair from the girl's clenched fist.

The plan was for them to ride the train around the diorama to see if they could find the mouse's hiding place. Once they knew where its den was, they would send an army to ambush it while it was sleeping. But the scouting force didn't come back. Somehow, the train had been derailed on the second level. A day later, a lone black terrier had come trotting back up the track, wagging its tail. The dog was dragging its leash, and the length of it was slick with blood and human viscera. There was no sign of the train's engineer, the soldiers, or the other dogs.

The majority of the diorama's citizens had chosen to stay in the city once they learned that a mouse was loose in the basement. Now that the train was derailed, and there was a man-eater hunting on the second level, they felt trapped. Already uneasy, the people started to panic.

A platoon of 50 men were sent to get my help, including the milkman, the farmer and the businessman. Their mission was to get the key from the workshop and get it upstairs. Once there, they had orders to mail three of the men and the skeleton key in one of the letters in the shoebox waiting by the front door's mail-slot. All the letters where addressed and pre-stuffed with a note, a matchbox that could hold three people, and a house key. They would try to reach me first. Then they would try my sister.

The soldiers never returned. But the mayor had a connection with the key and could feel its absence from the workshop. That, and the fact that no one had seen the key come flying back, meant that it, and at least one of the adventurers, had survived the trip to the mailbox, and the key was on its way to me.

Next, the mayor assigned the remaining builders and volunteers the task of constructing a wall around the island and blocking the train's entrance to the second level. They knew it would take a few days for the letter to reach help—even longer if the key came zipping back without me, and they had to mail it to my sister. Now, all they could do was wait, half hoping, half dreading the sight of the skeleton key blazing down the steps.

For the next few days, the builders frantically assembled a wall around the table. From the darkness around the island, they would occasionally hear screams. They told themselves it was the sound of an animal on one of the other tables. But it was possible that some people had snuck off the island to return to their homes. If that was the case, the screams implied they hadn't made it.

Some of the builders claimed they heard chewing sounds coming from the second level below their feet. Armed patrols sent to the second level didn't return, but faint screams would. Eventually the mayor stopped sending teams to investigate. Soldiers had stopped volunteering. He suspected that if he ordered them to go, he would have a mutiny on his hands.

By the fourth day, the builders were on strike too. They stopped working on the wall after a team saw something yank a man over the edge. A few lone workers had already disappeared. Their friends had assumed they'd abandoned their posts and were holed up somewhere in the town. After seeing one of their own desperately clawing at the wall and screaming for help, the builders realized that their missing co-workers hadn't been abandoning their posts after all. It was more likely they'd been torn away and then torn apart. The remaining builders put down their tools and quit as one. The mayor didn't blame them.

The inhabitants who were left were protected by the remaining soldiers, volunteers, and anyone else who could hold a weapon. They were armed with needles, sharpened nails, and shards of glass, huddled together in the buildings around the fountain and the inert statue of the town's hero. Every one of them was terrified, trying to stay silent, and now absolutely desperate for help to arrive.

Yesterday a few of them claimed they heard something large

moving around in the courtyard, sniffing at the building's thin cardboard walls, and then greedily drinking from the fountain. It had been too dark to see clearly, but someone peering through a clear plastic window saw a long tail—multi-colored in the faintly flickering Christmas lights—whipping in the air as a shadow disappeared around a dark corner. The eyewitness account of the shadow's size had to be exaggerated. Everyone was scared. People told stories. The length of the tail, the size of the shadow, grew in the re-telling.

Terrified beyond measure, they waited for two days in their hiding places. Staring into each other's eyes, smelling each other's fear, all quietly praying in earnest for the knight to save them once again. The creature was now prowling the streets of the town; the wall didn't stop it. It was only a matter of time before the creature realized it could chew through the thin cardboard walls they were cowering behind. Once that happened, their hiding place would become a charnel house.

The mayor, hiding on the upper floor of the courthouse, had been staring out the window, fixated on the basement stairs. After two long days, he saw it—the skeleton key—zooming toward the workshop. He frantically whispered the news to the others hiding with him, and moments later, the whole town knew. They heard my footsteps on the creaking stairs and then, blindingly, the sun lit up their world. That's when I saw them rush out of hiding, cheering their way into the brightly lit plaza. The heroes had returned, and soon the knight would be back too. They were saved.

I listened to the increasingly hoarse voices of the trio. By this time I had set down the tumbler, and I was resting my forehead on my weaker forearm, with my left hand cupped around my ear.

"I don't understand. How am I supposed to bring back the knight?" I whispered.

"The knight is already here," the mayor shouted with a wide toothless smile. He pointed up at the statue. "Take the knight to the workshop. Use the alcohol to clean it off and to soften the paints you find there. Then paint it with love. That's how our father brought all of us to life," the mayor instructed with what was left of his voice.

"He'll come to life, big brother; he'll save us," the milkman added. His voice sounded raw, and though he was speaking as loud as he could, I had to strain to hear him.

I looked at the heroic murals painted on the buildings, then at the metal statue on its platform. It was smeared with paint but stood proudly with its sword held high. I believed them. I knew what I needed to do.

With my left hand, I picked up the knight, hefting it for a moment, impressed by its weight. It was solid metal and easily half a foot in length. The sword was nearly three inches of blue-tinted steel, narrowing to hairline edges along both sides that looked sharp enough to shave with. I realized that to the inch-tall townspeople, the knight would seem like an indestructible giant, armed with a weapon that could cleave a mouse with a single stroke.

With my weaker arm, I picked up the tumbler, still filled with liquid from the bottle upstairs. It was a drink that wasn't for drinking. Tilting the glass, I examined its contents, watching it ripple and roll. It seemed to be glowing as it reflected the overhead light, the knight, and my wondering face. The sharp chemical smell bit at the air, an invisible cloud laced with memories of my father. Memories I now questioned.

So many times I watched him pour himself the same drink before heading to the basement. But had I ever seen him raise this glass to his lips? Maybe my father didn't love drinking. Maybe he hadn't been drinking at all.

With that thought, I turned toward my father's workshop. Behind me, the little people picked up their weapons and filed back into their hiding places. As before, they would wait, but now, in the light. They were waiting for me to bring their champion back—anointed with a fresh coat of paint and ready to slay the monster.

CHAPTER 4

RAGS TO RICHES

At the bottom of the stairs, next to the light switch, a sliding door painted blue led to the other side of the basement. It was slightly ajar, and I slid it open with my foot, flinching at the sound of the roller grinding on the track.

I was confronted with a surprisingly ordinary room; dim, dusty, bare. Half expecting to see more wonders, I don't know if I was disappointed or relieved. Scanning the large room with its concrete floor and cinderblock walls, I saw instead the everyday magic of a home's inner-workings: ductwork, pipes, a stout sewer line.

To my left was a paint-stained sink, and next to it a washer and dryer sitting side-by-side like boxy robots in love. In front of me was a bare laundry table, and a long, wooden bar loaded with tools. The far wall was filled with floor-to-ceiling cabinets with most of their doors cracked open or hanging slightly askew. In the center, the water heater and furnace stood together, looming like a two-faced industrial idol. In the shadows behind them, partially tucked under the stairwell, was my father's workshop.

Above the work space hung a row of shelves laden with books. Corkboard panels covered the rest of the wall, densely populated with photos, notes, and hand-drawn blueprints—except for a small space in the center. There, in a clearing among the paper, dangled the skeleton key. Previously pitted and black in my hand, the key was now a smooth, slate gray. It swayed side-to-side on its hook like a dog's tail tentatively wagging.

Under the sagging shelves and the corkboard's pinned foliage sat a wide drafting table. Spread across the table were newspapers, a pile of rags, and a scattering of art brushes, and tucked beneath, a low-backed bar stool and a couple wheeled carts with shelves packed full.

An adjustable lamp clamped one side of the table. It looked like a drooping metal flower, holding on at the base for dear life. Under the sad lamp was an antique wooden box with its lid flipped back and collapsible insides extended, creating a three-step stairwell rising toward the light. Small glass jars of dried-out paint lined the box inside, and a faded painting of an antique train wrapped around the outside.

I placed the knight and glass beside the box, sat down, turned on the light and pulled it toward me. In the dim room, the lamp was a harsh spotlight, and the knight laid beneath it like a body on a slab. I dipped a corner of a rag into the tumbler and wiped at the paint smeared on the armor, revealing the shining metal beneath.

As I cleared the paint away, I could see the incredible detail in the armor, with intricate chainmail, hinged joints, and movable limbs. I could tell there was an emblem on the knight's chest plate, but I couldn't make out what it was quite yet. I straightened its legs and arms, gently working the sword free from its delicate left hand.

Having gotten both arms straight at its sides, I froze. I could see now that the knight's right arm was shorter than the left and slightly twisted. I felt something twist inside me, a hot flush of confused emotion, like a fist in my sternum rising up.

Holding the rag in my stronger left hand and the figurine in my right, I rubbed hard at the paint-smeared emblem on its chest plate. The paint streaked and flaked away, revealing a tiny embossed image stamped into the metal—two hands clasped, one larger than the other. Together they formed the shape of a little lopsided heart. I leaned back from the table, my face hot from the lamp, eyes stinging from alcohol, and nose starting to run. The knight lay inert and heavy, a dead thing in my twisted hand. Now washed clean, its body shined like gold beneath the light—but its visor was still closed and caked with paint. The job wasn't done.

I leaned back in and re-wet the rag. As I cleared the paint away, I felt the visor move beneath the cloth. I pushed it up, knowing what I'd see—and there it was, a tiny replica of my father's tired face. His eyes were closed, his cheeks hollowed, his mouth a thin line. The same expression I'd seen him wear in his casket.

***

I had attended the funeral alone. My mother chose not to go, and my sister, all the way across the country with a newborn, couldn't make it. Self-conscious, I stood in the back of the sparsely populated room. The people there were relatives on my father's side, strangers to me, but some of them knew who I was and what my father had done. I felt them looking at me, and I was too aware that the right arm of my suit jacket hung loosely. My face burned with anger, shame, and other ill-defined emotions.

I remember feeling confused, like something impossible was happening. Like I was thrust into a suddenly unfamiliar world. The people standing right beside me seemed far away. I felt incredibly alone.

The service was absurd. The speaker didn't know my father any better than I did. The eulogies seemed like they had been written for someone else. I approached the casket toward the end of the service and stared down at the face of a stranger. He was a scrawny, pale reflection of the man I remembered less than fondly. The man I barely knew in life, in death, had become completely unfamiliar.

I felt something huge inside of me. A swelling in my throat, a pressure behind my eyes. I started to reach toward my father with my left hand, reaching out, I guess, for the last time. Then, realizing what I was doing, I let my hand fall limply to my side. My right hand, a sweaty ball in the pocket of my suit jacket, was clenching and unclenching rhythmically, like a heart beating. My fingernails dug into my palm, like a handful of tiny nails, like an animal's gnawing teeth. Then I turned and walked away with my chin lowered, my mismatched fists clenched, and my uneven shoulders slouched.

I didn't look back.

***

Now, here in the basement, looking at the knight's face, I felt like I was back in the funeral home and teetering at the edge of an invisible cliff. I set the damp cloth and knight down and clumsily and repeatedly wiped my hands on my thighs. I wanted to help the tiny people in the next room, but this was all too strange and happening too fast—like a train picking up speed, one that at any minute could go flying off the tracks. But it's not easy to stop a train. They have their own momentum.

I grabbed a handful of the little paint jars and rolled them across the table like dice. I twisted open three of the lids, and using one of the paintbrushes, added a few drops from the tumbler into each jar. I started painting.

Not being much of an artist, I made a bit of a mess of it, but I did the best I could. I carefully painted the knight's helmet, gauntlet, and boots green, his chest plate and sheath orange, and his chainmail blue. As I brushed on the paint, I tried not to look at the figurine's face, and I tried not to think about my father in his casket. I failed on both accounts.

Soon I was done, and the brightly painted knight lay under the light—not moving. As I had painted the stiff limbs I felt panic coiling within me, I had suspected that the "magic" wouldn't work. I was right. The knight lay there motionless. I had failed.

I leaned back and let the paintbrush fall across the knight's body like a dropped flag. My left hand fell to my side. Under the harsh white light of the lamp, I looked at my right hand, clenched in frustration next to the knight. It looked like a child's fist.

Right then I remembered what the mayor said: Paint it with love. That's how your father brought all of us to life. I wasn't painting with love. I couldn't. The basement, this strange adventure, was revealing something I had feared, a truth I hadn't wanted to acknowledge to myself.

I didn't love my father.

I didn't feel the things a son should feel. There was nothing there. As much as I hated the numbness, the coldness in my heart, that's all I had in the place where the love for a father should be. Whatever bond we had was broken, never healed, and over the years my love had withered away.

I sat staring blankly at the knight, the clumsily applied paint, and the mess I'd made on the table. I noticed the oddly pink tint to the formerly white light from the lamp. The color of the light had changed. I glanced up. Above the lamp, the skeleton key was glowing a bright neon red, and it was no longer swinging back and forth. It was defying gravity, hanging horizontally, like the hand of a clock at 3:00. It was pointing at something tacked to the corkboard—a folded piece of notebook paper, and on it, in my dad's familiar handwriting, was my name.

I stood up and yanked the note off the wall. As it came free, the thumbtack popped off and rolled across the table, bringing a photograph down with it too. It drifted like a leaf to the table, image-side down between the body of the knight and my clenched hand. Above the desk, the key—now a bright yellow—resumed its tentative back and forth sway. Moving with a little more force now, wagging less tentatively.

I unfolded the note.

Son,

I'm sorry I hurt you. I was protecting my world. It's your world now. You are its hero.

Love,

Dad

It was all too much. I sat back on the stool and rested my head in my hands, bracing myself before flipping over the yellowing photo that fell to my father's desk. The photo he worked beneath when he painted with love and brought the inhabitants of his world to life.

It was a photo of the two of us.

My sister took it the summer before she went to college. She had gotten a camera that spring and and had carried it around everywhere. In the photo, we were sitting on the edge of a fountain at a fair held a few towns over. The town, I suddenly realized, on which the diorama was based. In the picture, my dad's arm is around my shoulder, and my left arm around his waist. He was looking down at me with unmistakable love and warmth.

In the photo I'm waving my smaller and twisted right hand at the camera unselfconsciously, my fingers and face powdered with sugar from a funnel cake the two of us had shared. There was a little powdered sugar on my dad's face as well. With our tousled hair and sugar goatees, we looked like twins separated by a few decades. No, not twins. We looked like father and son.

I looked down at the knight that looked so much like my father. It also looked like me. I glanced back at the photo and stared at the man who had been a mystery to me, a mystery I'd not wanted to solve. He wasn't such a mystery now. I'd seen the secret he had been trying to protect, and I had an idea of what it cost him. I understood my father better now. I admired what he created. I forgave him for what he'd done trying to protect it. I pitied him for what it had cost.

I felt something unfold inside of me and I started to cry. A hot rush of emotion, filled my eyes and spilled over my bottom lids. Sitting there, surprised by grief, I wept for my father and my family—for what we lost, what we hadn't shared, and for what could have been.

Tears dripped off my chin and the tip of my nose, falling onto the newspaper, making dark, spreading circles among the bright smears of paint. Then, still crying softly I looked at the knight and saw a single blurry tear drip off the tip of my nose and land squarely on the knight's face.

Its eyes opened.

CHAPTER 5

COMEDY

Suddenly, I was simultaneously looking down at the small knight lying on the table, and I was on my back looking up at the tear-stained face of a giant. I was the knight. I was the giant. I was in two bodies. I was seeing double. I felt like throwing up. I felt like getting up.

I effortlessly hurled off the paintbrush laying across my breast-plate like a two-by-four and scrambled to my feet. Standing up, I watched in amazement as my larger body, looming over the table's horizon, went limp and started to slide off of the stool it was sitting on.

Feeling my larger body starting to tip, I frantically seized control of it and grabbed the table's edge to keep myself from pitching over onto the basement floor. As I tried to keep myself on the stool, I watched the knight collapse like a puppet with its strings cut.

Okay. I understood how it worked. I could control both bodies—but I couldn't manage two bodies at once. Fighting dizziness, I lay down on the basement floor next to the stool, shut my eyes and opened the knight's.

I sat up fluidly and looked down at my paint-smeared armor. I examined my gauntleted hands. The left opened and closed at my command, the right was a smaller solid ball of steel in the shape of a fist. The knight was disabled, like me. Still, I was used to only having full use of one hand. This wasn't a problem. I felt powerful. I could feel a vibrating tautness in my limbs, a solidity and strength unlike anything I'd ever felt before. My entire body was dense metal, but I could move with the confidence and grace of an Olympic athlete. This was amazing.

I got up effortlessly, in complete control of this marvelous body. With a single fluid motion, I scooped up my sword and slid it into the sheath on my back. I walked to the edge of the table and looked down. Far below, I could see my other body sprawled out on the floor—huge, soft, and weak.

Without hesitation I leapt from the table onto the stool, then stepped backward over its edge. I dropped four inches straight down, reached out, and wrapped my arms around the leg. Holding it tightly with both arms, I slid down it like a fireman's pole.

I landed lightly, crouching with my right fist supporting my weight on the floor of the suddenly, impossibly large basement. When I landed, my fist sunk down in the floor, up to my wrist. I must have landed harder than I thought. When I pulled it up, I left a hole the size of a pencil eraser in the concrete.

I looked up at my big, unconscious body, then lay down beside it and closed my smaller eyes. After a disoriented moment, I opened my larger eyes and whooped out loud with joy. I was myself again! The basement was its normal size. I sat up slowly and burped, wincing at the hardness of the floor against my elbow and the nausea I felt from the sudden shift in perspective. My eyes were gummy, and I had a string of drool on one cheek.

I felt terrible, sick, sluggish and heavy, and as I rose to my feet I swayed unsteadily. I was painfully aware of my weaker side, an aching knee, my belt buckle digging into my stomach, a stuffy nose, slight pain in my lower back, my teeth felt weird, and there was a bad taste in my mouth. Compared to the fluidity and grace of the knight's body, my real body felt awful. I wanted to be the knight again.

I picked up the knight, smiled widely with two mouths, and headed toward the other side of the basement. As I picked it up, I could feel my smaller body rising up into the air, but as I paid attention to that feeling, I felt a wave of vertigo. Staggering past the HVAC unit, my larger body listed to one side and nearly careened into the sink before I regained my balance.

I was figuring this out. I needed to get my smaller body to the trainset without collapsing. To do that, I must ignore what it was feeling and carefully put one foot in front of the other. I knew my smaller body was tough, but I didn't want to drop it. Plus, I didn't want the townspeople's first sight of the cavalry to be my huge figure stumbling in, falling flat on my face, and dropping their hero to the floor. The thought of such an anticlimactic moment made me laugh out loud, and as I made my way through the diorama room, that was the sound they heard as I carefully set the knight down in the center of the plaza. Still dizzy, I lowered myself to the cold basement floor, smiled up at the island, closed my eyes, and opened them in my father's world.

The room expanded outward in all directions. In the blue sky, cotton clouds hung suspended. Model plains made wide lazy loops around the ceiling fan's light and blurred yellow blades. On the ceiling, Christmas lights sparkled and blinked. They were hung in a widening spiral starting at the light fixture and extending outwards to the edges of the room. Their cords were painted the same blue as the sky and the flashing bulbs seemed to float in the air like multicolored UFOs, moons and planets. Stuck to the ceiling behind them was an explosion of faintly luminescent glow-in-the-dark stars, comets, ringed planets, and spiraled galaxies.

I turned my head and saw the intricately painted cobblestones, the vast expanse of the plaza, the toy houses, the buildings, and the people tumbling out of them like children dismissed for recess. It was all perfect. It was all beautiful.

My visor was up and I could feel a breeze on my exposed face. Next to me, I could hear the water splashing in the fountain. I could also hear the sound of the rapidly approaching crowd. I rose to meet them, effortlessly, as though assisted by invisible strings. They rushed toward me, none taller than my knees. Each was a unique work of art, in costume, with arms extended and hands spread wide, looking up at me with precious faces painted with wonderful attention to detail. All of them laughing, talking excitedly, smiling, and some crying with joy.

I greeted them with laughter and tears too.

Eventually things calmed down, and I got to talk to the mayor one on one. We sat beside each other on the fountain's edge—him swinging his legs, me towering over him and sitting gingerly, with my hands resting on my thighs. When I first sat down, my right hand brushed against the edge of the fountain and a sliver of stone had flaked away. But the mayor had assured me it could hold my weight and enthusiastically patted a spot next to him.

"You should watch where you swing that thing, big guy," he said, laughing.

I laughed too. Charmed by his painted face with its squinty eyes and gummy smile. Charmed by the way he had ordered the crowd to give us some room, while shaking a finger like a cartoon character, and by the way they happily obeyed. The crowd, likely too far back to have heard the mayor's raspy comment, joined in on the laughter.

"We love having you here, but you can't stay long. The longer you're here, the worse you'll feel when you're out there again," he said, gesturing with one hand toward me and the other to where my body lay beyond the horizon. He looked at me inquisitively, his head tilted and his face a wrinkled map of concern. I think I understood. I remembered how terrible I had felt in the workshop when I'd returned to my body after being in this one for just a few seconds. I had already been here for a few minutes. I shuddered. Maybe it would be a good idea to move fast.

"You, me, those two, and the mutt," he said gesturing to the milkman, the farmer, the child, and the dog, all waiting on the other side of the square. "We'll go down to the under land together, and you'll put the train back on the track. I'll drive it back, and the dog will help the three of you find and kill the monster." The mayor looked up to meet my eyes, his chin jutting out and his toothless mouth in a firm line which comically seemed to cave in the bottom half of his face.

I reached back and lightly touched the hilt of the sword sheathed on my back. I glanced across the plaza at the mural of my dad grappling with the two mice.

"I'll need help finding it—but I won't need help killing it," I replied with a grim smile.

A mouse might seem huge to the townspeople, but it would be about the size of a large dog to me. I was easily twice as big, made out of solid metal, and wielding a sword half my size. No more townspeople would die on my watch.

"I'm here now. Everything will be okay," I said, loud enough for the crowd to hear. They roared with approval. The dog weighed in with a series of short barks. He sounded like he was trying to tell us something. The mayor, the milkman and the farmer all looked at him for a moment and then started to laugh. I joined in.

"Let's go," I said with a smile, and I gently scooped up the mayor, holding him in the crook of my right arm like a baby. With my other hand, I drew my sword. The gesture was so quick and instinctive that it felt like the sword unsheathed itself and leapt into my hand. The milkman and the farmer, who both had sharpened nails strapped to their backs, drew their weapons as well. We were ready. The girl kneeled and put a leash of red string around the dog's neck, then handed the other end to the farmer. The dog's tail wagged with a purpose. He was raring to go.

The small girl then turned to me with solemn eyes and held up a piece of paper for me to see. I squinted to see a crude drawing of a mouse. Well, the way the mouse must have looked to her. A mouse as a monster. She'd drawn a picture of herself fighting it. In the picture, she had on gold armor like mine and was wielding a sword, facing off against the creature, easily four times her size.

Three tiny bodies and a black speck lay strewn in the background. The girl there stood alone beneath the looming monster, hopelessly outclassed, still fighting.

I smiled at the little warrior, amused that she wanted to join us and flattered that she had drawn herself as her hero—as me.

"You can't come with us, it's too dangerous for a kid. But if it wasn't for you, we wouldn't have the monster's scent. We wouldn't be able to do this without your help," I said softly, filled with pity for this fatherless child. I couldn't bring her father back, but I sure as hell could avenge him. Looking into her imploring eyes, I wished I could do more.

The child didn't reply. She just held up her drawing. We left her by the fountain, standing with the paper rippling in the breeze like a defaced flag. The four of us walked through the adoring crowd, following the dog to the subway station where the tracks descended to the level below.

I ducked my head as I descended the ramp, and the mayor wrapped his arms around my neck. The underside of the table was painted the same light blue as the walls and ceiling. It was dim, but there was ambient light, and from the top of the ramp I had a good view of the entire level. I didn't see the mouse. There didn't seem to be any kind of theme to this level at all. It was a juxtaposition of regions and times, some of which I'd seen from the bottom of the stairwell. It was picturesque but strange, and its silence and emptiness made it even more so. It looked like a really well-organized toy box, maybe that's what the whole diorama was. No, toys don't die, this diorama was something else entirely.

Ahead of me, the track passed by a medieval castle, a small village, and a dense forest of gnarled trees. A third of the trees had been gnawed to splinters; the rest had craggy faces carved into their trunks. The faces were all frozen in expressions of terror. Next to the forest was a cross-section of a cavernous region sculpted out of clay. The stalactites and stalagmites were covered with primitive versions of the town's murals. Next to them was the futuristic city. In the city's depths I could see lights flashing faintly. Next to the city, two aquariums flanked the track. Both had model boats bobbing on their surfaces. At the bottom of one was the sunken pirate ship I'd seen earlier, and in the other, a sunken submarine sat solemnly at the bottom.

The part of the table I'd been unable to see from the stairwell, featured a Parisian cafe, its table and chairs all upturned, and a collection of European landmarks—the Eiffel Tower, Big Ben, The Globe Theatre. Beside that, a spread of farmland densely dotted with model trucks and tractors, farmhouses, barns, and silos. That's where the train had derailed. It was lying on its side, and its boxcars were scattered behind it on both sides of the track. Still in my arms, the mayor gestured that way, and the dog, tugging urgently on its leash, seemed to concur.

"Put her on the track, and reconnect the cars. I'll take it from there," the mayor said into my ear as the four of us approached the train. It looked easy enough. The train was large to them, but to me it was about like lifting a mattress. I lowered the mayor to the ground, sheathed my sword and got to work.

While the mayor, milkman, and farmer watched in awe, I lifted the train and carefully aligned its wheels with the track. Then I reconnected the nine cars one by one, lifting them easily. They were hollow metal boxes that to me felt like moving a few tall filing cabinets. As I moved them into place, I noticed the two at the front had slightly indented sides marked with colorful graffiti. Tiny little tags of hard-to-read names in bubble letters. Did they have a graffiti problem in the town? Tiny little gangs? I chuckled to myself as I connected the final boxcar and caboose.

"All aboard!" I said, turning to the group with a smile. They weren't smiling back. As I'd been connecting the last car, the mayor opened the door to the driver's cab, and just as I turned toward them, the engineer tumbled out. His neck was obviously broken, and two sightless eyes stared from the bloody, pulpy mess of his face. The mayor staggered backward in surprise as the limp body landed at his feet. The farmer was beside him to help him into the cab, and he had the presence of mind to keep the mayor from falling.

The milkman kneeled beside the engineer's body.

"This happened when the train derailed," the milkman said in disbelief. "His face probably hit the glass," There was a catch in his voice. The engineer was his friend.

"Why did it derail? This is a straight shot," the farmer said, panic in his voice. He surveyed the stretch of track in both directions as if expecting to see a holographic reenactment of the crash.

"He was probably trying to get away from the mouse and went too fast. The real question is, where are the soldiers and the dogs?" The milkman replied, as he closed the engineer's eyes.

"I'll take the train back to town and come back with reinforcements. Not that I think you'll need them, but maybe you'll want to see some friendly faces and get a ride back after you've killed that thing," the mayor said from the doorway of the train's cab. His face was ashen as he leaned against the doorframe for support. He nervously wiped his mouth with one shaking hand as he looked up at me.

"Thank you for your help, but you've got to pick up the pace. Pretty soon, you'll have been here too long," he added, and with that, he shut the door. A moment later, the train started up and pulled away, slowly picking up speed as it rolled up the track. Within moments, it had passed the ramp descending from the first level and entered the forest, disappearing from sight.

Unnerved by his parting comment, I looked down at my two remaining companions. They were both looking at the dog, who had wandered off to a neighboring farm. It was pawing at the ground, tail stiff and fur bristling. It wasn't barking though. It was absolutely silent.

"Mutt's got something!" the farmer yelped, his voice equal parts fear and excitement.

CHAPTER 6

OVERCOMING
THE MONSTER

We jogged over to see what it was. The dog didn't seem to
have a trail; it was just digging at the ground. I wondered if it had
found the burial site, then I remembered where I was and recalled
my first sight of the island as the taller version of me. There was a
level below this one, covered in cobwebs and dust, crowded with
supplies and junk. If I were a mouse, that would be where
I'd hide.

I looked down at my companions, and they looked up at me.
The milkman pointed down and raised his eyebrows. I nodded
slowly. The farmer looked at us both in confusion, started to ask

something, and then his eyes widened. He got it.

"That's where the spiders are," he said softly, with fear in his voice.

"I'm not worried about spiders. I'm going over the edge," I whispered. "You two stay here with the dog and wait for the mayor's reinforcements. Tell them what we've discovered."

"I'm coming with you," the milkman whispered fiercely. "I'm not taking no for an answer. You kill the mouse. I'll kill any spiders we see. Plus, someone needs to witness the battle—how else will the artists know what to paint?" He glared up at me, his arms crossed and his mouth a tight line with just a hint of a smile.

That last point was a hard one to argue with. He was hard to argue with. He'd been with me for this whole adventure. I wanted him with me at the end too.

"Hang over the edge by your hands. I'll reach up and pull you down. Sound good?" I whispered back, smiling.

He understood, put his nail in his strap and walked with me to the edge of the table. I laid on my stomach and peered down to the third level. It was even darker than the second. Viewing it upside down, the entire level was a crowded labyrinth of junk buried under a blanket of dust. I didn't see any spiders, thankfully, but their webs laced the bottom of the table and drooped from the ceiling, obscuring the view.

Still, I could make out the area below where the dog had been digging. It was near the middle of the table behind a row of paint cans. Through a gap between two of the cans I could make out what looked like a partially flattened building, one that would be the perfect size for a mouse to curl up in.

I knew where to go, I knew what to do. Once I saw the mouse, it wouldn't be able to get away. I sheathed my sword, grasped the edge of the table one-handed and, ever so gently, lowered myself onto the bottom level. I was in perfect control of this body, and I landed softly without making a sound. I helped the milkman down as well, kneeled beside him and drew my sword, pointing it toward the area where I suspected the mouse's lair to be.

"If it runs, I'll catch it. You won't be able to keep up. Don't try. Rejoin the farmer, and wait for the mayor or me to return," I whispered.

He nodded that he understood, his eyes two bright spots in the gloom, staring up to meet mine. Then he drew his sharpened nail, and we entered the dark maze. I had a mental image of the route we needed to take. We walked beneath a canopy of spider webs that brushed against my face and shoulders, and we stepped carefully through the fog of disturbed dust that drifted up to the milkman's waist.

We navigated between two plastic bins that loomed on each side of us like impossibly smooth cliffs—one packed with sewing supplies, the other filled with rolls of wrapping paper made color-less in the low light. Beyond the bins, a package of paper towels stood next to a string of Christmas lights, which were tangled like a briar patch bearing multi-colored fruit. Behind the lights were the paint cans, and behind those, our destination.

As we passed the paper towels I felt the milkman lightly touch the back of my knee. I turned to see him pointing toward a section of the towels that had been completely shredded. Nearly half of the rolls had been reduced to chewed-up scraps. The string of lights, too, had been chewed in multiple spots. Around us the dust had been disturbed, and faintly I could smell the hint of something wild in the air.

The milkman held up one finger and shook his head vigorously. He then held up two fingers, three, four, five, and widened his eyes, his face gray from dust or fear or both. I understood what he was trying to tell me. This didn't look like the work of just one mouse - this was a full-blown infestation.

I flattened myself against one of the paint cans, the milkman right beside me. We listened carefully for any noise, and faintly, from the other side of the cans, we heard something moving.

I knelt down next to the milkman and put my face to his ear. "Stay here. But if you need help, run toward me," I breathed. Then I stood up, crept forward, and peered around the curve of the can.

I saw a horror.

In the deepest shadows, underneath a canopy of spiderwebs,

was destruction. I recognized this discarded section of the diorama from the mural: a crushed row of buildings, a smashed water tower, and the damaged replica of my father's house. It was faded with age and covered with dust, blood—and bodies.

I stared at the house I had crushed as a child. Its wall had collapsed, its roof sagging and half torn off. Squirming in its depths, in a bed of shredded paper and filth, were the bloated bodies of almost a dozen mice—each easily a third of my size. Their hairless pink bodies writhed and twisted around each other like a clenched fist of misshapen fingers. In the midst of them and their filth, I could see the rotting remains of partially devoured men, women, and children.

The mice seemed to be waking up. They were moving clumsily, and sniffing at the air, but their eyes were closed. They looked half asleep. Now that I was here, they wouldn't have a chance to wake up.

I hurled myself at them, swinging my sword in a long, low sweep that split one in half, beheaded a second, and gutted a third. I expected them to retaliate, but the remaining mice still seemed sluggish and confused. I took advantage of their disorientation and swung my sword in another long arch—tearing out the throat of another and severing another's spine.

The remaining mice started to scream and scramble away. I kicked one back and hacked another into two squirming pieces. One threw itself at me and was impaled on my blade. Thrusting forward, I impaled another, using my foot to scrape them both off my sword. The remaining three mice attempted to run. I brought my sword down on the back of one fleeing, cleanly severing its spine, then I lopped off another's screaming head.

The last mouse caught my eye as he rushed straight toward the milkman. I lunged at it, swinging my sword down like an axe along its length. The mouse split cleanly in two and its guts exploded, splashing at the feet of the shocked milkman.

"Are you okay?" I asked, smiling as I kneeled beside him and wiped my blade on the severed flank of the carcass at our feet.

The milkman didn't answer. He was looking behind me, his face frozen in shock. I glanced over my shoulder and saw, out of the darkness, the headless body of the farmer floating toward us. Before I could react, a huge shape detached itself from the shadows—it was the real monster, carrying the farmer's corpse. Impossibly high up, two glowing eyes burned.

They were staring at me.

It was a rat, easily four times my size. Standing on its hind legs, its head scraped against the ceiling. As the farmer's body dangled in its mouth, I realized the rat was bringing it back to the nest to feed its babies. The baby rats I had just hacked to pieces.

"RUN!" I shouted at the milkman, then wheeled around, bringing up my sword. The rat dropped the farmer, half screamed, half roared, and lunged forward, slamming into me. I heard the impact more then I felt it, and I flew backward into the row of paint cans. I smashed into one head-first and found myself lying on my back with my sword arm lifted above my head at an odd angle. The rat reared up again, turning toward my companion. The tiny milkman scrambled to get to his feet, slipping and sliding in a puddle of blood.

I'd managed to hold onto my weapon, but it was stuck in the can of paint. I yanked it free, and red paint gushed out, drenching both my sword and the left half of my body. I leapt up to hurl myself at the rat. But something was wrong. My left leg was stiff, and my sword arm hung limply at my side. I no longer had control of my left side. The red paint had somehow canceled out my father's magic.

I compensated, lurching forward on one leg, and slammed into the body of the rat just as it reached for the milkman. The two of us skidded across the table and flew over the edge. As we toppled, I saw my other body sprawled across the basement floor below, its serene face upturned.

I fell straight down, landing flat on my face. My left arm was a flopping, inert mass, and I had lost my sword. My left leg was still useless too. I tried to push myself up off the paint-streaked floor with my right arm, and for a moment I thought it had snapped clean off, then I saw that it was embedded up to its elbow in the concrete. I desperately yanked it free and looked around wildly for the rat.

I saw with horror that it had landed on the chest of my other body and that its paint streaked body was crawling up towards my exposed throat and face. I screamed and slammed my small eyes shut and opened my other eyes wide.

The rat exploded in size, and I was suddenly staring directly at its black shining eyes, its yellow teeth, and its twitching, blood-streaked muzzle. It was on my chest—mere inches from my face, and scrambling up. I could feel its claws tearing my shirt, scratching the skin beneath. I tried to scream and spewed vomit instead, coughing it up on my shirt and the rat.

I scrambled back, desperate to get away from its teeth, its claws, and its feverish weight on my chest, undeterred by the vomit. I tried to swat it off, my legs kicking and arms flailing, and then, THUNK—I cracked my forehead against the bottom edge of a table. I felt a bolt of pain accompanied by a white flash. I opened my eyes to find I was suddenly in the body of the knight again, weaponless, half paralyzed, and watching my huge body slump bonelessly to the ground with a gash on its forehead. I saw my body hit the floor and my head bounce against the concrete with a sickening hollow sound. My face was a bloody mask turned toward me, its eyes open and unseeing.

Still clinging to my chest was the enraged rat with its teeth bared. It sniffed the air, smelling the blood from my bleeding forehead and continued climbing up to my exposed throat, my slack face, and my open, sightless eyes.

Slipping slightly in the paint, I managed to haul my smaller body up, balancing precariously on one leg. My control over this body was fading fast. Half of it didn't work, and the numbness was spreading everywhere the red paint touched. I blinked hard, trying desperately to see through my other eyes, but there was nothing there. I was stuck in this half paralyzed, off-balance body.

The rat was on my other body's face now, its claws digging into my cheeks, its fat bloated body covering my nose and mouth. I saw that body start to twitch and convulse. It was suffocating, and so was I. I could see darkness creeping in from the corners of my smaller eyes.

I screamed at the rat and staggered to my larger body. We were half paralyzed, suffocating, weaponless, dying. Faintly, I heard the milkman shouting. I turned to see him leaning over the edge of the diorama. He held up his right hand in a tight fist.

"Brother! Use your weapon! Use it!" He cried out, his voice raw, his eyes desperate.

But I had dropped my sword. My left arm and leg were dead. All I had left was the single leg I was standing on, and the mis-shapen ball of my useless right hand—so much like the clenched fist he was holding up in the air.

My mind flashed back to the workshop. To the eraser-sized hole I'd left in the concrete when I'd landed. To the piece of the fountain I'd accidentally chipped away.

"You should watch where you swing that thing big guy," the mayor had said, laughing.

I remembered moments earlier, after falling off the island, how my clenched fist had sunk into the concrete up to my elbow.

My large body convulsed again. The rat, eagerly lapping at the gash on my forehead, shifted on my face. One of its claws was rested on my lower eyelid, almost touching the exposed white of my eye. Its back claw was caught in the corner of my slightly open mouth, creating a half leer beneath the rat's suffocating weight. The rat lifted its bloody muzzle, sniffed at the air, and then it opened its mouth wide, revealing long yellow incisors smeared with my blood.

"Brother! Use your weapon!" The milkman screamed again. His voice sounded far away. The light was retreating too.

I looked down at my clenched misshapen hand as the dark spots multiplied in my vision, and suddenly I understood. It wasn't a handicap—it was a bludgeon. It had been my weapon all along.

I kicked off with my right leg, launching myself toward the rat. I flew higher and farther than I thought I had the strength for. It turned and rose up to face me. Its claws spread wide, its eyes glowing, its gaping maw roaring, the fur of its muzzle and body clumped and clotted with my blood. It loomed huge in the center of my fading vision as, with the last of my strength, I brought my fist down squarely between its eyes.

Its head exploded.

Blood, teeth, and brains sprayed in all directions, and we fell together. I tumbled to rest beside my larger body, my vision fading. The last thing I saw was the headless body of the rat flopping down on the floor beside me, then darkness.

CHAPTER 7

REBIRTH

After that, things got a little fuzzy. I remember opening my eyes and looking up at my mom's concerned face. She was out of focus and doubled in my vision. Behind her two faces, the ceiling light blazed like the sun, with a halo that pulsed in sync with my pounding head. She shook my shoulder and dabbed at my forehead with a wet cloth. I closed my eyes.

I remember her helping me up the stairs. She cried and said something about finding my father passed out on the basement floor a few times as well.

She helped me into her car, and as she shut the door I remember yelling at her to make sure the front door was locked. It hurt my head to yell, and I drifted off again.

I woke up in a hospital bed with my head bandaged. It felt like I had a brick strapped to my forehead. My mom told me where I was and how I had gotten here. She had stopped by to pick up my father's mail when she saw my car in the driveway. She came in to see what I was doing and found the basement door open and the light on. She went down to investigate and saw me and the dead rat. "Honestly, it was as big as a cat," she said. We lay side-by-side on the floor in what she at first thought was a puddle of blood.

It scared the hell out of her. When she got closer she saw that the blood was unusually bright, and that it was flowing from the bottom of the island, or, as she referred to it, "that damn trainset of your father's." A paint can, not her son, had burst open. Still, I was a mess. I had a knot on my forehead, my whole face was bloody, I had thrown up on myself, and I reeked of alcohol. She said that last part worriedly.

She'd managed to wake me and get me to her car. "There's red paint all over the seats," she added with a shudder. She also said the basement door had swung shut behind us and locked when we left. Thankfully I had the key. She'd seen it on the bedside table and assumed I'd put it there.

I glanced over at the table. The room spun sickeningly. It hurt my head to turn. The key was there, all right. Shining brightly in the sunlight streaming in from the window. The last time I'd seen it, it had been swinging on the hook in my father's workshop. I had left it there—yet here it was.

I told her I just poured a tiny drink in honor of my father and went down to look at the trainset. The rat surprised me, and I had chased it around the basement, swinging the metal bowling trophy that my dad had placed in the center of the diorama. Somehow, I managed to corner the rat against some paint cans on the bottom level and crush its head with the trophy. Then I slipped in the paint from a can I accidentally spilled, and falling, I almost crushed my head too. I'd managed to give myself a pretty good concussion at least. The summary was mostly true, and she didn't pry further. I was grateful for that. It hurt to talk.

Eventually she went out in the hall to talk to the nurse, and I was alone. Something rattled on the bedside table—the key. Okay, maybe I wasn't totally alone. I suspected it was mine now. I bet it would be for a while.

I leaned back in the bed and closed my eyes. The pain went away, and I could feel a breeze on my face and the weight of my sheathed sword across my back. I opened my smaller eyes to my clenched right hand shining brightly and raised triumphantly toward the light in the robin's egg blue sky.

I surveyed the plaza. It was a bustle of activity, filled with small figurines in brightly colored costumes, all going about their day. Occasionally a figure would stop and smile up at me. Across the plaza, on the side of one of the buildings, I could see a new mural in process. It was partially obscured by toothpick scaffolding, but from what I could see, it looked like a masterpiece of the knight caving in the head of a rat four times his size.

I looked down and saw that a father and daughter sat together on the edge of the fountain. No, not a father and daughter—it was the milkman and the small dark-haired girl. He wrapped his arm around the girl's shoulder as he smiled to himself and stared dreamily into the blue sky at the circling model planes and cotton clouds. The girl was busy drawing a picture—the knight with its arm raised in victory. The little black dog was there too; its head cocked and tail wagging as he attentively watched the girl's vision come to life. All three of them looked happy. I was happy too.

I opened my larger eyes in the hospital room. I could hear my mom talking softly with the nurse in the hallway. My body still hurt, but my head had stopped aching. I smiled up at the ceiling, my eyes wet. Faintly, off in the distance, I think I heard a train whistle blowing.

Made in the USA
Lexington, KY
14 November 2019